I Would Eat
His Heart
in the Marketplace

Jamie Lackey

Cover Image: *The End of the Quest* (1921) Frank Bernard Dicksee
Public Domain in United States

Book Design: Todd Sanders

ISBN: 979-8-9850216-4-6

I Would Eat
His Heart
in the Marketplace

To my Aunt Vicky -
Thank you for your love and support and for your shining
example of everything an aunt should be.
I'll do my best to follow in your footsteps.

Sometimes, when Beatrice first woke up in the morning, her loneliness sat in her chest like a wound. An old, familiar wound, dull and aching and endless. She allowed herself to trace the lacy surface of her armband, imagining the damning letters of her soulmark beneath the fabric. The words that someone would speak to her in the moment she knew she loved them.

"Enough. I am engaged."

When she was young, she imagined possibilities beyond the obvious. She dreamed that she wasn't doomed to fall in love with someone pledged to marry another.

But as she grew older, her ability to lie to herself faded. She eschewed the entire idea of romance. She could be perfectly happy without it.

On such mornings, she let herself wallow in her sadness for the space of three breaths. Then she made herself get up. Get dressed. Smile and be merry.

She was perfectly happy.

Benedick didn't like waking up alone. Luckily, being Don Pedro's right-hand man meant that he was in charge of guard rotations, and he was able to make sure that his schedule aligned with whoever his current lover happened to be. So on this campaign, he woke up to a sleepy Count Claudio every morning.

Benedick knew that he should be happy. They'd captured the prince's bastard brother Don John. The fighting was over, and it was time for some well-eared relaxation. But Benedick wasn't made for peace.

He poked Claudio's shoulder. "Wake up."

Claudio wrinkled his nose adorably and made a small sound of protest.

Benedick poked him again. "We make for Messina today."

"Messina?" Claudio repeated, finally opening his eyes and blinking sleepily.

Benedick nodded. "Messina. Don Pedro wants to visit his friend Leonato." He was just so cute. It wasn't fair. Benedick took a deep breath. "So we should probably put an end to this."

Claudio sat up, suddenly awake. "What are you talking about?"

"We agreed that our relationship was temporary," Benedick said. That was something he was always clear on at the beginning. All of his relationships were temporary. "Now that the campaign is over, I thought you might like to move on. Find someone else."

Claudio's eyes went cold. "You mean you're ready to find someone else."

Benedick laughed. "Who in Messina, of all places, could compare to you?"

"Then why now?"

Benedick's gaze flicked to Claudio's armband, then to his own. He was getting too attached. Too used to Claudio's sleepy morning expressions, too used to the way he felt in his arms. And getting attached would only lead to heartbreak. Claudio wasn't for him. Claudio would find his soul mate, and they'd probably be just as adorable and sweet as he was.

Meanwhile, Benedick's fated love was insane. And clearly, he was, too. Why else would he fall in love with someone as she said, "Would that I were a man! I would eat his heart in the marketplace."

Claudio sighed. "This is about your soulmark and your sad feelings about it."

"I suppose it is."

"You know, even if someone were to speak my words, I could still choose you. If you'd but let me."

Benedick sighed. "Who am I to stand in the path of true love?"

Claudio's face darkened. "You're set in this, then? Nothing I say can convince you?"

"Please, let us be done and remain friends," Benedick pleaded.

A single tear rolled down Claudio's cheek, leaving a gleaming trail behind it. Of course he would even cry prettily. He took a deep breath, and turned his shining eyes to Benedick. "I am no great believer in soulmarks. And I love you. But if you leave me now, I will do my best to concede to your wishes, and turn my sights to other loves."

Benedick brushed the tear from Claudio's cheek, kissed him once, softly, on his sweet lips. Then he left him behind.

And if he cried when he reached his own room—ugly, painful sobs, well. That would stay his secret.

🦋

Beatrice sketched a strawberry blossom, plucked for her study. It would live on in charcoal, but never complete its transformation from flower to fruit. She refused to feel any affinity to it.

"Cousin, look, is that a messenger?" her cousin Hero squinted into the midmorning sun. The girl needed spectacles, but refused to wear them, claiming they gave her headaches.

Beatrice suspected she just didn't like the way they made her dewy eyes appear smaller. She shaded her eyes and looked. "Indeed, and he is approaching quickly."

"Perhaps he has word of when Don Pedro will arrive," Hero said, clearly delighted at the prospect.

Beatrice fought to keep a scowl off of her face. But maybe the news would be good. Maybe the avowed heartbreaker and eternal bachelor Signior Benedick had been tragically lost. Not killed, for that felt too cruel to wish for. Just left behind in a cave somewhere.

It galled her that Benedick as a bachelor was acceptable to society, but if she chose not to marry she would be a pitied tragedy. He could go on adventures and take lovers and she could only stay by her cousin's side and draw.

Not that adventures or lovers sounded particularly appealing to her, but she would prefer the freedom to choose.

"Good morning!" the messenger cried as he approached.

Beatrice's Uncle Leonato finally looked up from his book. "Oh yes, it is a good morning. The light is very fine today."

"I am to tell you that Don Pedro and his party are fewer than three leagues out, and will be arriving soon."

"Excellent, excellent. And tell me, have you lost anyone in the recent action?"

The messenger shook his head. "No sir."

"Excellent news! We will prepare to welcome the whole party. I hear that Don Pedro has bestowed much honor on a young Florentine called Claudio."

"Indeed! He has borne himself beyond the promise of his age, doing in the figure of a lamb the feats of a lion."

Hero heaved a dreamy sigh, and Beatrice rolled her eyes. Benedick had clearly not been abandoned in a cave, which was deeply disappointing.

"How goes Signior Benedick of Padua?" Hero, the nearsighted menace, asked.

"He's returned, and as pleasant as ever he was."

Beatrice laughed at that description. Pleasant? Benedick? That could not stand. "I pray you, how many has he killed and eaten in these wars? Or rather, how many has he killed? For I promised to eat all of his killing."

The messenger blinked at her. "He has done good service, lady."

Leonato shot Beatrice a look. "You must not, sir, mistake my niece. There is a kind of merry war betwixt Signior Benedick and her. They never meet but there's a skirmish of wit between them."

Beatrice caught the warning in her uncle's speech, but refused to back down. "In our last conflict four of his five wits went halting off, and now the whole man is governed by but one. Who is his companion now? He seems to have a new 'sworn brother' every month or two."

The messenger's lips twitched. "He is most in the company of the right noble Claudio."

Beatrice placed one hand on her forehead. "God help the noble Claudio! If he has caught the Benedick, it will cost him a thousand pounds before it may be cured."

The messenger gave a startled laugh. "I would not cross you, lady. But I should be returning to my lord."

Leonato sighed. "Let us go and prepare for Don Pedro's coming." He positioned himself between Hero and Beatrice, taking each of their arms in one of his. "We shall all do our best to be civil, shall we not, girls?"

Hero laughed, as if she hadn't been the one to mention Benedick's name in the first place. Beatrice gave her uncle a merry smile, and no promises.

Benedick let no trace of his heartache show on his face, even when Claudio moped about, giving him significant looks. Benedick did not meet his eyes.

Leonato's house hadn't changed since he'd last seen it—it was a noble edifice, well-maintained and comfortable. A warm, welcoming place. It was unfortunate that it housed the worst harpy of his broad acquaintance.

And there she was, standing next to her uncle. The sun bright upon her hair, her countenance cheerful, her bearing regal. His eyes were drawn to her against his will, and he could scarcely look away. She was a beautiful lady. It was such a shame that her face and personality were so poorly matched.

Don Pedro strode forward, grinning. "Good Signior Leonato, you are come to meet your trouble. The fashion of the world is to avoid cost, and you encourage it."

Leonato stepped forward to meet him, his hands outstretched in welcome. "Never came trouble to my house in the likeness of your grace."

"And this must be your daughter."

"Her mother has many times told me so."

Benedick couldn't resist that opening. "Were you in doubt, sir, that you asked her?"

Leonato laughed. "Signior Benedick! No, for then were you a child."

Benedick couldn't help laughing in return. "I do recall your wife as a great beauty, sir. Your daughter must be glad to take after her, she would surely not wish for your face."

"I wonder that you will still be talking, Signior Benedick. Nobody marks you," Beatrice said.

It was unfair that her voice was as lovely as her face, both of them disguising her black heart. "What, my dear Lady Disdain! Are you yet living?"

Beatrice arched a shapely eyebrow. "Is it possible disdain should die while she has such food as Signior Benedick? Courtesy itself must convert to disdain, if you come into her presence."

"Then courtesy is a turncoat. But it is certain that I am loved by all, only you excepted. Would that I could find any tenderness in my heart though, for truly, I love none."

He expected a flinch from Claudio at that, but his ex-lover didn't react.

"A dear happiness to all. They would else have been troubled with a pernicious suitor. I thank my cold blood for this one similarity between us. I would rather hear my dog bark at a crow than a man swear he loves me."

"Thank the heavens for that. Some gentleman or other shall escape a scratched face."

"Scratching could not make it worse, if it was a face like yours."

Don Pedro cleared his throat, loudly. "Signior Claudio and Signior Benedick, my dear friend Leonato has invited us all to stay with him, and we shall stay here at least a month."

Leonato, the kind old codger, turned to Don John, who Benedick had been doing his best to ignore. "Let me bid you welcome, my lord. Being reconciled to the prince your brother, I owe you all duty."

Don John nodded as if such was his due, and not at all like he was grateful that his neck remained unstretched. "Thank you."

Everyone moved toward the open doorway, but Claudio clutched at Benedick's hand. His heart softened. Maybe another month or two of dalliance wouldn't be the worst idea.

"Benedick, did you see Signior Leonato's daughter?"

Benedick blinked. "I did not note her, but I saw her."

"Doesn't she seem like a lovely, modest, and kind young lady?"

"She didn't even open her mouth," Benedick protested. "You can't judge kindness based on appearance, just look at her terrible cousin."

"I'm serious. What do you think of her?"

He was serious? Benedick had told him to move on, but he hadn't expected him to latch onto the first woman he saw. "She's too low for a high praise, too brown for a fair praise and too little for a great praise. I do not like her."

"Don't be jealous," Claudio said. "She is the sweetest lady that I have ever looked on."

"I can see yet without spectacles and I see no such matter. Her cousin, if she were not possessed with a fury, exceeds her as much in beauty as the first of May does the last of December."

Claudio sighed dreamily. "She is like a dream come to life. Could all the world buy such a jewel?"

"Yes, and a case to put it in," Benedick snapped.

Don Pedro emerged from Leonato's door. "What secret has kept you two here?"

"Claudio has had his heart stolen," Benedick said, pride keeping all bitterness out of his tone.

"Oh? And who is this clever thief?"

"Hero, Leonato's short daughter." Benedick felt he had achieved a major victory by keeping his commentary to her height.

"The lady is well worthy," Don Pedro said. "I will facilitate a meeting for you to speak, so that you may perhaps exchange words. It is possible that she is your fate." He clapped Benedick on the shoulder. "And perhaps we will find someone here for you, as well. I know how poorly loneliness suits you."

Benedick imagined shoving every one of his feelings into a box, then imagined burying the cursed box in the desert. "As you say, my lord."

Beatrice was braiding Hero's hair when Leonato swept into the room they shared. "My daughter, I have news." He took one of Hero's hands between both of his. "One of our men overheard Claudio and Don Pedro speaking in the courtyard, and it seems that young Claudio has fallen under the spell of your beauty."

Hero's face lit up like the sun, but Beatrice felt an unwelcome jolt of sympathy for Benedick, being so thoroughly cast aside.

Though perhaps the rumors were wrong, and Benedick had another companion. From what she knew of Benedick, he could have half a dozen.

"If the prince arranges a meeting, you must speak freely and openly to Count Claudio. Be warm and kind, and surely your words will match his skin. For who could know you and not love you, my perfect daughter?"

"As you will, Father. I will do my best."

He kissed her forehead. "Of course you will."

He left them again, and Beatrice attended to her cousin with the utmost care. "You will not be too sad if I leave you for my marriage bed?" Hero asked.

Beatrice employed her sunniest smile. "Miss you? Hardly. You snore like an old dog, I will rejoice in the silence of my solitude."

"I would see you happy, Cousin."

"You see me happy every day, Cousin."

"Do I, though?" Hero asked. "You think your mask is perfect, but I know you well. I see the moments it falters."

Beatrice blinked back traitorous tears. "Seeing you happy would bring me great joy. Would this arrangement make you happy?"

Hero grinned. "It very well may. Claudio is very handsome. We will see how the meeting goes. I confess I hope for it to go well."

"I am sure of it. Your father is right. No one can know you and not love you."

Hero hummed happily. "Did you hear about Don John?"

"That he is a traitor lucky for his brother's mercy?"

Hero rolled her eyes. "That he is unmarked, and that is the root of his misery and anger."

Beatrice sometimes wished herself unmarked. It seemed like a fine freedome. But she could also see how the lack could lead to resentment. To know that there was no one you were destined to love. No one destined to love you in return. "That is no real justification for treason."

Hero shrugged. "If the prince can forgive him, it is not for us to judge. It must be hard, seeing others enjoy something you know you will never have."

Beatrice rubbed her armband. "Yes, I suppose it must."

Benedick was avoiding both Don Pedro and Claudio, and succeeding in that, but he hadn't been mindful of where Leonato put Don John, and stumbled into him and his duo of cronies plotting in the hallway.

In the hallway! Didn't the man have a room to lurk in?

Don John was too involved in his ranting to notice Benedick, who froze like a mouse spotted by a hawk. "I would rather be a canker in a hedge than a rose in his grace, and it better fits my blood to be disdained by all than to try to rob love from any. In this, though I cannot be said to be a flattering honest man, it must not be denied that I am a plain-dealing villain. I am trusted with a muzzle but I have decreed not to sing in my cage. If I had my mouth, I would bite."

"What exactly are you threatening to bite?" Benedick asked, unable to help himself. "Are you a rabid dog, ready to turn on the hand that feeds you?"

Don John spun to face him. He didn't have his brother's noble looks, but he was not displeasing to the eye. Just to the soul. He met Benedick's gaze and sneered. "Do not get above yourself, Signior. You claim my brother's love, but Claudio stands above you. And I hear you once claimed the most exquisite Claudio's love, but now he has chosen another as well."

"You keep his name out of your mouth," Benedick snarled.

"Is it true, that he hopes to win the fair Hero? To woo and wed her, exchanging marked words as well as vows?"

"Perhaps he does. It is none of my concern."

"No? It doesn't make you angry, that he has moved on so quickly and completely?"

Benedick shrugged. "It was I who ended things, so I have no right to such complaints."

"Noble words, but do they truly match what is in your heart?" Don John took a step closer. He smelled of smoke and leather with just a hint of something sweet. Orange blossom, perhaps? It turned Benedick's stomach. "Perhaps you'd like to see their proposed union come crashing down? To have young Claudio retreat back to the safety of your arms?"

"I want no part of your schemes," Benedick said. "I should get to supper."

Don John arched an eyebrow at him. "I will be dining in my room with my companions." He reached out and trailed a finger across Benedick's cheek. "You would be welcome to join us."

Benedick recoiled. "I know my reputation is impressive, but let me tell you clearly. I do not dally with those that I do not care for, and I will never care for you."

"I doubt my darling Conrade or dearest Borachio could win you over then, either. But our door is open, if you do ever change your mind."

"You said it yourself earlier, sir. You are a villain."

"And it is only a Hero who can win hearts?"

Benedick wished he was still on the battlefield and could strike him. "Take care," he said, turning on his heel. "I take my leave of you now. Enjoy your dinner."

"You too," Don John called after him.

Benedick gritted his teeth. He hated giving anyone the last word, but he was at his limit.

And now he was off to dinner, where Hero and Claudio would be sitting and smiling at each other.

At least Beatrice would provide a distraction.

Beatrice loved little more than a party, and her uncle threw a brilliant gala to welcome the prince and his men. She danced and laughed and jested. Claudio and Hero were cloistered off on their own, hesitant smiles drawing out reticent blushes.

"They talk in circles, each trying to prompt the other. How long do you think it will take for them to exchange words?" Benedick asked, his shoulder brushing against hers.

"You seem in poor humor tonight, Signior."

"And you seem disdainful as ever. You know, I think I have found the source of your wit. Are you familiar with the *Hundred Merry Tales?* I hesitate to accuse you of plagiarism, but the similarities speak for themselves."

Beatrice glared at him. "Behold, the prince's jester, a very dull fool. His only gift is in devising impossible slanders. None but libertines delight in him; and the commendation is not in his wit, but in his villany, for he both pleases men and angers them, and then they laugh at him and beat him."

"Is that a threat, lady?"

"Verily it is not. But I have no desire to battle with you tonight. It is a time for dancing."

Benedick took her hand. "Very well. We'll dance, then."

"Nay, Signior, I was not asking you. I will go and find myself another partner, one who does not vex me."

"Beatrice. Please."

The sound of her name on his lips, worryingly, did not displease her. She glanced again at Hero and Claudio, then at Benedick. By the look on his face, he had indeed been cast aside. Pity stirred in her heart. "Very well. One dance, and only because you look like you might die from misery if I refused. Never again can you claim that I am not a creature of kindness and mercy."

He danced well, and she found herself laughing from the sheer joy of the movement and the music and the warmth of his touch.

The prince claimed the next dance, and she smiled at Benedick as she whirled away from him.

He smiled back, and she nearly tripped, and clutched Don Pedro's arm to steady herself, and laughed again.

Don Pedro smiled down at her, and this time her footing remained true. "In faith, lady, you have a merry heart."

"Yes, my lord, and I thank it. It keeps on the windy side of care." She glanced over at Hero and Claudio as Claudio brushed an errant lock of hair back behind Hero's ear, and Hero rose up onto her toes to kiss him on the cheek. "Look. My cousin tells him in his ear that he is in her heart."

"So she does, I'm sure. Has your cousin ever confided in you her marked words?"

Beatrice shook her head. "We keep such things private in this house. I have shared my words with no one. And I doubt I ever will. I may sit in a corner and cry for a husband, but that is not my fate."

"Lady Beatrice, I will get you one."

Beatrice shook her head. "I would rather have one of your father's getting. Have you a brother like you? Your father got excellent husbands, if a maid could come by them."

The prince considered her for a long moment. "Will you have me, lady?"

Beatrice gasped and her heart stuttered in her chest. If her uncle had heard whisper of this possibility he would have urged her even more fiercely than he had Hero. But of course Don Pedro could not be serious. She managed an easy smile. "No, my lord, unless I might have another for working-days. Your grace is too costly to wear every day. But, I beseech your grace, pardon me. I was born to speak all mirth and no matter."

They danced in silence till the prince smiled again. "Your silence most offends me, and to be merry best becomes you. There is no question that you were born in a merry hour."

"No, my lord, for I'm sure my mother cried. But then there was a star that danced, and under that was I born."

The dance ended, and Beatrice sought a less draining partner. She was quite finished with heavy conversation for the night.

Hero and Claudio continued to murmur together, and suddenly Claudio let out a joyful cry and pulled down his armband, showing her words she must have just uttered.

One set was more than enough for the match to move forward, for everyone knew that love did not always proceed at an even pace. Her uncle and Don Pedro huddled together, clearly making plans for the upcoming union.

But none of that was Beatrice's problem. She would dance until she was so tired that not even Hero's snores could keep her awake.

"She said my words, and I felt it like an arrow through my heart," Claudio said, clinging to Benedick's arm. His eyes shone like stars.

He was beautiful.

Benedick forced a smile. "That sounds like such a pleasant sensation. You'll forgive me if I don't rush to follow your example."

"It is interesting that she has said your words, but you haven't yet discovered hers," Don John said, sliding into their conversation like the snake he was.

"She offered to show her words to me, that I might read them," Claudio said, his voice dreamy, "But I want it to happen naturally. I am willing to wait and woo her, to win her heart honestly."

Don John hummed. "Is it possible that she learned your words beforehand? If she was willing to let you see her words unearned, she must be desperate for your goodwill. Perhaps she is acting so at her father's urging?"

The light in Claudio's eyes flickered. He turned to Benedick. "Think you that could be the case? Could she be luring me in for a political alliance, and not be acting from her heart at all?"

Benedick glared at Don John. He had had a trying night. Beatrice had misused him past endurance. What right had she to such a beautiful smile. And contrast that to her words. The prince's fool? An absurd accusation. He was often merry, and felt no shame in it. He was sure he was not known far and wide as a fool. It was due to Beatrice's base and bitter disposition that she could think him so.

And so what if she did dance so well? And so what that her perfect laugh, so like the pealing of distant bells, seemed to lodge itself in his chest? And so what if Don Pedro had looked at her with something like longing? He was welcome to her, if he could win her. Which he doubted any man could. She was as wild as the most dangerous horse. And twice as deadly.

Benedick wrenched his mind back to the present. "How could she have discovered your words? Not even I have seen them." That was a lie—Claudio's painfully inane words were, "I am very fond of grapes." Claudio was not particularly careful of his armband, and it sometimes slipped, revealing the marked skin beneath. But thinking of Claudio's skin was no comfort. It still hurt to be replaced so quickly.

Don John glared back at Benedick, but Claudio's light rekindled. "You're right. It was foolish of me to doubt. Clearly she is my destined other half." He heaved a great sigh. "If only we could marry tomorrow!"

At that, Don John rolled his eyes so hard that Benedick hoped he might hurt himself. Then the prince's brother turned his attention to Benedick. "And wherefore are you sad, Siginior?"

Benedick dearly wished that Don John would silence his infernal mouth. "I am not sad, my lord."

"Sick, then?"

"No," Benedick said curtly.

Don John leaned into his personal space. "You are neither sad, nor sick, nor merry, nor well, but civil. Civil as an orange, and something of a jealous complexion."

Benedick generally loved to be around other people, but in this moment he wished himself a hermit. Would that he could go a month, nay a year, without seeing any of his current companions' faces.

"Are they truly so horrible, your words?" Don John asked. "I have wondered for some time. I suspect they indicate that your soulmate is a woman, since it is known that you give your smiles to both ladies and gentlemen, but never more than that to any lady, no matter how sweet."

"I wonder why you'd take such trouble to put any thought into it at all," Benedick said, fighting down a flinch.

"It is a common question in camp," Claudio said, and Benedick wondered why he had ever cared for the boy. "I confess that I am myself quite curious."

Benedick covered his armband, even though it was safely beneath his sleeve, and no gentleman of any sort would dream of tearing it from him. His hands were shaking. In anger, surely.

"You know, of course, that I am unmarked myself," Don John said, his voice suspiciously soft.

"It is no surprise, since clearly you lack the capacity to truly care for another, to value someone else above your own interest."

Claudio gasped, but Don John smiled, unbothered by Benedick's insult. "But is that any better than what you are doing, running from your fate as hard as you can?"

Benedick's hands curled into fists, but Claudio grabbed Benedick's arm and pulled him away. "It is late. By your pardon, my lord."

When they were safely away, Claudio released Benedick's arm. "What were you thinking, letting him get to you like that?"

Benedick gaped at him. Did he not remember that he himself had nearly let Don John convince him that Hero's affections were a nefarious ploy?

Benedick spotted Don Pedro in the hall ahead of them, and hurried to join him. "Will your grace command me to any service at the world's end? I will go on the slightest errand now to the Antipodes that you can devise to send me on. I will fetch you a tooth-picker now from the furthest inch of Asia, discover for you the location of the holy grail, fetch you a unicorn hair, or even serve as an emissary to the fairies, rather than stay any longer within these walls. Please, do you have any employment for me?"

"None, but to desire your good company."

"My company this night is nothing but bad. I will part from you and hope I find myself better in the morning."

He left Don Pedro and Claudio in the hall, watching him with what looked distressingly like worry. Don Pedro leaned down and spoke in Claudio's ear.

He left them to their whispering.

They had no cause for worry. A good night's sleep would set him right.

At least he certainly hoped it would.

Beatrice maintained that she was acting perfectly normally. She only seemed sad and out of sorts next to Hero and her maid Margaret, both of whom flittered about and giggled over nothing all morning. "I know what has put Hero into such a distressingly happy state, but what in the world has gotten into you, Margaret?"

The maid blushed and looked to the floor, but her lips refused any shape but a smile. "It's nothing, lady. I'm just pleased to see Lady Hero so happy."

"Impossible. You have your eye on someone yourself, don't you?" Margaret's blush deepened. "No, you're right. Tell me nothing of it, for I cannot bear to hear another word on love. I'm going to go to the orchard."

She gathered her charcoal pencils and paper and went forth. Some sketching would do her a world of good. It was a lovely morning, and it would be a shame to waste another moment of it on thoughts of other people's romance.

She was well involved in examining the fall of sunlight across the honeysuckle and wondering how exactly to capture the feel of it when she heard her cousin and Margaret approaching.

Hero's voice shattered her focus. "No, truly. She is too disdainful. I know her, and her spirits are as coy and wild as the wind."

"But are you sure that Benedick loves Beatrice so entirely?" Margaret asked.

Beatrice dropped her pencil.

"So says the prince and my new-trothed lord."

Impossible. Benedick loved her? He didn't even like her! Beatrice knelt to reach for her pencil, and if it hid her behind the honeysuckle, so be it. Honestly, she had told them where she'd be, if they did not wish for her to overhear they shouldn't be speaking of such things in the open air.

They seemed to have paused in the shade for their conversation, and Margaret's voice came no closer. "And did they bid you tell her of it?"

Hero sighed. "They did entreat me to acquaint her with his feelings, but I persuaded them that if they loved Benedick, they should wish him to wrestle with his affection, and never to let Beatrice know of it."

Beatrice gripped her pencil with white-knuckled hands.

"Why did you do so? Does the gentleman not deserve Beatrice's affection?" Margaret asked.

"I know he deserves as much as may be yielded to a man. But nature never framed a woman's heart of prouder stuff than Beatrice's. Disdain and scorn ride sparkling in her eyes, devaluing what they look on, and her wit values itself so highly that to her all other matter seems weak. She cannot love."

The honeysuckle swam in front of Beatrice's eyes, and she wiped away tears of anger. They must be of anger, for she'd allow herself no other emotion. Did Hero truly think her incapable of love?

Margaret hummed. "You may be right. And therefore certainly it would be bad if she knew of his love. She would make sport at it."

"Why, you speak the truth. I never yet saw a man that she could not find fault in. She delights in disparaging things others praise. If a man is fair-faced, she would swear the gentleman is too pretty and could be her sister. If he is tall he looms. If he is clever or amusing he tries too hard."

"Such carping is not commendable."

"No, but who would dare tell her so? If I should speak, she would mock me. She would laugh me out of myself, press me to death with wit. Therefore let Benedick consume away in sighs and waste inwardly. It would be a better death than to die from mockery."

"Yet I still think you should tell her of it and hear what she will say."

"No," Hero said, her voice firm. "Rather I will go to Benedick and counsel him to fight against his passion."

"Lady, do not do your cousin such a wrong! She cannot be so much without true judgment. We all know that she has such a swift and excellent a wit, and only a fool would refuse so rare a gentleman as Signior Benedick."

So rare a gentleman as Benedick? Absurd. Perhaps he did dance well. And no one could argue that he didn't have a handsome face and fit form. And he was clever. And amusing. And tall.

Hero sighed. "He is the only man of Italy, except for my dear Claudio."

With that, their conversation turned to Claudio's many fine qualities, and they continued their walk, their voices fading as they walked away.

Beatrice blinked away more tears. The smell of honeysuckle hung thick in the air, and the sunshine suddenly felt too bright, her whole body too hot. Did she truly stand condemned for pride and scorn so much? Did Hero truly think she could not give her honest criticism for fear of mockery? Had she let her fear of her soulmark poison all of her relationships?

It wasn't romantic, but it was also not uncommon to simply reveal your soulmark to your chosen person, to let them read the words aloud. Of course, that risked someone else saying them naturally someday. But with words like hers, that was no real threat.

She imagined Benedick sliding her armband down to her wrist, tracing the words on her skin. His smile as he read them aloud.

Goosebumps danced down her spine.

He really did have a very charming smile.

Very well. Let no one say that she could not change, that she resisted growth, that she valued spite above happiness. "Farewell, contempt! And adieu, maiden pride," she said, standing up and brushing off her skirt. "Love on, Benedick. I will requite you, taming my wild heart to thy loving hand."

Benedick did feel somewhat better in the morning. He loved mornings. Everything was so fresh and clean and new. Though he felt a momentary pang at the loss of Claudio's sleepy smile. He watched the sun rise and ate a private breakfast in his room, then borrowed a book from Leonato's library to read out in the orchard. It was too fine a day to spend it indoors.

Would that he could go riding. But the temptation to simply turn his horse toward the horizon and keep going might prove too strong to resist, and his honor required that he remain.

The orchard would have to do. He picked a spot under an apple tree, leaning his back against its strong bark. Snowy blossoms, tinged with pink at the edges, lent sweetness to the air and comfortable shade to his chosen spot.

He spotted Leonato, Claudio, and Don Pedro walking along. He had no desire to speak with them or anyone, so he ducked behind one of the shorter apple trees, hoping that its low branches would hide him.

The prince did not call out to him, so he assumed that his plan was successful.

"Come hither, Leonato. Are you serious in your news that your niece Beatrice is in love with Signior Benedick?" Don Pedro asked.

Benedick choked on air. Luckily, the other men seemed to not hear him.

"I never would have believed that Lady Beatrice would love any man," Claudio said.

Leonato nodded. "No, nor I. But it seems most disconcerting that she should so dote on Signior Benedick, whom she has in all outward behaviors seemed to abhor."

"Perhaps she counterfeits love?" Don Pedro suggested.

That made more sense that Beatrice loving him, but what could motivate such an act?

"There was never counterfeit of passion that came so near the life of passion," Leonato protested.

The prince's eyebrows climbed up his forehead. "Why, what effects of passion shows she?"

Leonato coughed. "What effects? Hmm. What effects. Claudio, my daughter must have told you."

"She did indeed."

"How, how, pray you?" the prince asked again.

Claudio hesitated for a long moment, then leaned in and whispered in the prince's ear.

Don Pedro leaned back, shock clear on his face. "You amaze me. I would have thought her spirit had been invincible against all assaults of affection."

"I would have sworn it had, my lord. Especially against Benedick."

Benedick wished he had heard what Claudio had whispered in the prince's ear. It must be quite a sign of love to be met with such a reaction.

"Has she made her affection known to Benedick?" Don Pedro asked.

Leonato shook his head. "No indeed, and she swears she never will."

Claudius ran his hands through his hair. "Hero confided in me that Beatrice told her, ‹Shall I, who have so often encountered him with scorn, now write to him that I love him?' and Hero agreed that it did seem impossible. She says that Beatrice will begin to write to him, that she'll be up twenty times a night, and there she will sit in her smock till she has written out all of her feelings, but then she will tear each letter into a thousand pieces."

"Indeed," Leonato agreed. "She railed at herself, that she should be so immodest to write to one that she knew would flout her. "I measure him,' says she, "by my own spirit; for I should flout him, if he wrote to me, even though I love him, I would."

Benedick found himself nodding. A confession between him and Beatrice was indeed impossible. Even if they both truly loved each other, their history of discord would make them both too wary to trust, too eager to lash out.

"Then down upon her knees she falls, weeps, sobs, beats her heart, tears her hair, prays, curses. 'Oh sweet Benedick! God give me patience!'"

Benedick hoped that Claudio was exaggerating. The thought of Beatrice weeping on her knees out of love for him left him feeling unsteady. And like a villain second not even to Don John.

Leonato nodded sadly. "She does indeed. My daughter says so. And Hero is sometimes afraid she will do a desperate outrage to herself."

They were silent for a long moment. Benedick felt sick.

The prince tapped his chin thoughtfully. "Perhaps it would be good for Benedick to learn of it from some other, if Beatrice cannot tell him."

Claudio scoffed. "To what end? He would but make a sport of it and torment the poor lady worse."

Benedick choked again, this time on a protest. His behavior was never so deplorable!

"She is an excellent sweet lady, and virtuous," Don Pedro said. "Surely even Benedick must see that."

Claudio nodded. "And she is exceedingly wise."

"In everything but in loving Benedick," Don Pedro said.

"I am sorry for her, and wish there was something I could do, being her uncle and her guardian. But the situation seems impossible on all sides."

"I would she had bestowed this dotage on me," the prince said. "I would marry such a lady in a heartbeat. But I pray you, let us tell Benedick of it, and hear what he will say."

Benedick nodded. Clearly, telling him was the most reasonable path forward.

Leonato hesitated. "Do you truly think it a good idea, my lord?"

"No," Claudio cried. "Hero thinks surely she will die. For Beatrice says she will die if he doesn't love her, and she will die before making her love known, and she will die if he woos her."

"Perhaps she is wise to hide her love. It is very possible that Benedick would scorn it. As we all know, he refuses anything like a real commitment, preferring to flit from one fling to the next," the prince said.

"He is honest in his relationships, and kind to his lovers," Claudio said. "Though it is painful to try to breach the walls around his heart and be pushed back, he is cheerful and witty and wise and valiant. And has varied and practiced skills to ensure his partner's needs be met."

"Shall we then go seek Benedick, and tell him of Beatrice's love?" Don Pedro asked.

Claudio shook his head. "No. Never tell him, my lord. We must counsel Beatrice to master her heart. Benedick will never want it, and will refuse it coldly if it is offered. I know this from firsthand experience. I love him well, but I do wish that he would modestly examine himself, to see how much he is unworthy of so good a lady."

The dinner bell sounded, and they all turned toward it, leaving Benedick cowering alone behind his apple tree.

He covered his face with his hands and took slow, deep breaths. He felt the sunshine on his skin, smelled the apple blossoms and freshly turned dirt. He thought of Don John's accusations the night before and Claudio's most damning last words.

He had never wondered if Claudio had cried when Benedick left him behind. Had never considered that he might have left a trail of broken hearts in his path. For he had always been clear on the temporary nature of his affections, and surely most of his partners had embraced the same. But some, like Claudio, had tried to give him their true love, and he had spurned it every time.

"Good heavens but I am a callous monster," he confided in his tree. "But if Beatrice loves me, it must be requited. It is as they said. She is truly too good for me. She is fair and wise and virtuous." If anyone could read his soulmark words and laugh, it was her. She was a merry creature, and they could be happy together. They would be happy together, he vowed it. He placed his hand over his armband. "I know that I swore that I would never marry, but when I said I would die a bachelor, I simply did not think I should live till I married."

He could delay going in to dinner no longer. How could he face Beatrice? How could he broach her thorny defenses and confess that he was hers, body and soul?

He had never tried to win someone's heart before.

Beatrice herself emerged from the trees, like his thoughts had summoned her. She was truly beautiful, a vision of grace. He had always known it, but hadn't ever really allowed himself to see it before.

They stood in silence for a long moment, regarding each other.

"I am sent to bid you come in to dinner," she said. He thought he did detect some softness in her tone.

"Fair Beatrice, I thank you for your pains."

"I took no more pains for those thanks than you take pains to thank me. If it had been painful, I would not have come."

Benedick fought back a smile. "Then you take pleasure in the message?"

He couldn't read Beatrice's expression, and he stifled the impulse to reach for her hand. It was too soon. "Just come and eat, Signior." Was that fondness in her voice?

"Lead on, and I will follow you."

Beatrice was growing certain that she didn't understand love. Hero and Margaret were so happy. They walked about as if they floated on a cloud comprised of nothing but butterflies and the laughter of babies. But Beatrice found love to be a painful thing, like a thorn wedged into her heart. She couldn't look at Benedick without it aching. When he smiled she found it hard to breathe. Certainly that wasn't normal?

And she couldn't ask Hero for advice, because then her cousin might suspect that Beatrice had eavesdropped on her earlier conversation. Or accuse her of counterfeiting her feelings.

She had been hardly able to control her voice or face when she'd been sent to fetch Benedick for dinner. She'd found him standing beside an apple tree, shrouded in blossoms, looking thoughtful and handsome. Her fingers had itched to sketch him.

Perhaps that was an answer. Surely such a request would flatter him, and spending time together quietly, hopefully without verbal barbs, could be a key first step.

Yes. It was a good idea. She would try it. The only question that remained was how to approach him with the invitation.

Hero appeared at her elbow. "Cousin, Claudio and I are going to go for an after-dinner stroll. Pray, come with us to chaperone."

"You are to be married in two days, do you truly require a chaperone?" But Beatrice let herself be pulled along. They met Claudio at the gate, a reluctant Benedick at his heels. How well he looked in the gentle light of the setting sun.

"Surely you don't need both of us," Benedick said. Beatrice wondered if he was well, for he appeared a touch flushed.

"Oh, come with us for a walk," Claudio said. "It'll do you good. You are a man of action, and not made to be moping about within four walls."

"I have not been moping," Benedick grumbled. Then he sighed and looked to Beatrice. "Do you not object to my company on this outing, lady?"

"It is kind of you to worry about my preferences," Beatrice said. She tried to keep her tone even, but was afraid it came out awkward. Or worse, tart. Or maybe awkward was worse. "But do as you will, surely you do not need my permission."

"For if it were in your power, you would forbid me to breathe?" Benedick asked.

Beatrice laughed. "We are not so short on air that I begrudge you your share, Signior, even if you do claim more than your fair portion."

She wondered again if Benedick was unwell. He looked poleaxed. Surely her response wasn't that out of character?

Hero and Claudio had walked on, hands intertwined. "Come," she said, "we must follow our leaders."

"In every good thing," Benedick said, sounding vaguely out of breath.

Beatrice smiled at him. "Yay, but if they lead to any ill, I will leave them at the next turn."

"And abandon me to chaperone them on my own? I'm not sure I'm up for the task."

"Speaking of tasks," Beatrice said, feeling her cheeks heat. "I have a request for you."

"Ask it, lady," Benedick said. He sounded serious, almost grim.

"Would you be willing to sit for me to sketch you?"

Benedick tripped over his own feet and fell at hers. He gaped at her from the ground. "What... what nature of sketch? If I may ask?"

Beatrice frowned at him. "I simply thought you looked quite picturesque by the apple blossoms earlier. But if you do not wish for me to sketch you, simply say so. There is no need to make a jape out of it."

Benedick scrambled to his feet. "I meant no offense, lady. It was simply an unexpected request. I am honored. Truly."

Beatrice considered. It hadn't gone badly. In fact, she could have honestly expected it to go much worse. She nodded. "Very well. Meet me tomorrow morning, in that same spot. Now come, your gymnastics have given our charges quite a lead."

Benedick stared at the ceiling over his narrow bed. Beatrice wanted to sketch him? Did she seek some token of him, something to keep with her when he was gone? She would need no such thing, for he vowed that he would never be parted from her.

But that put proof to it. She loved him. There was no possibility of doubt.

What did one wear to be sketched? He blushed again at his first thought, that she'd been requesting that he pose nude. Of course she would not have considered such an impropriety. She would expect him decently clad. Should he don his full uniform? Or something more casual?

Perhaps, once they were married, he would pose for her wearing nothing but a smile.

He pushed that thought firmly aside and willed himself to sleep. He needed his beauty rest. It would not do to face Beatrice with bags under his eyes.

In the morning, he considered every bit of clothing he had with him, and ended up dressing much as he normally would.

Beatrice had arrived before him. She had set up an easel and was examining her pencils. She glanced up at him and gave him a tiny smile. It wasn't an expression he'd seen on her face before. If he didn't know any better, he would think her nervous.

But then, that must be it. She was afraid that he'd notice her regard, that she'd betray her heart by some careless word or lingering look. He remembered how desperate for secrecy she had been in her quoted speech to her cousin.

Benedick would do nothing to betray his knowledge. He had her heart, but he must prove that he was worthy of it, that he wouldn't mock or hurt or scorn her.

And he'd start by doing exactly as she requested. "Where do you want me, lady?" he asked.

"Stand over there, near the flowers." Beatrice's voice was all soft command, and it sent shivers down Benedick's spine. "Yes, just there. Now turn toward me, just a bit. Perfect. Tilt your head up. No, no, not like that. Like this." She demonstrated how she wanted him to tilt his head, drawing out the fine line of her elegant neck.

Benedick tried to emulate her, feeling somewhat ridiculous.

"That's good."

Her praise was like a drug, and he was glad that she doled it out so sparingly. Any more than that would have incapacitated him.

"Are you comfortable? Do you think you can hold that pose? Don't nod, just say yes or no. And try not to move your jaw when you do."

"Lady, I have fought battles. I can stand still for a bit."

Beatrice smiled like a cat. "You may find it harder than you expect. Still, I thank you."

She fell silent, and the only sounds were the birds greeting the day and the faint scritch of her charcoal across canvas.

Seconds stretched. Benedick's nose itched. A fly viciously attacked his ear. His back started to ache and his shoulders grew stiff.

The sun had not moved an inch away from this horizon.

"This is torture," Benedick said.

Beatrice laughed. "But you have fought battles! Surely you can stand in one place for five minutes."

"It cannot have been any less than an hour," Benedick said. "You and the sun are conspiring against me, I see through your trickery."

"Hold still."

"What are your plans for the drawing, once it is finished?"

Beatrice held out her pencil and closed one eye. "I enjoy the act of drawing, but think little of my pieces once they are complete. Why? Do you want it? Perhaps you could put it up in your room to admire your own visage?"

"Or perhaps instead I would admire the quality of your work. But you are right, I have no need of a sketch of myself, if I long to see my own face I can simply seek a mirror. But perhaps as payment for my time, you might give me a different drawing. One that I may post and admire."

Beatrice seemed taken aback by the request, but nodded. "That seems fair, I suppose."

"I am well known as a fair man," Benedick said.

"Your hair does shine prettily in the sun."

Benedick's cheeks grew hot. He should not be so pleased to hear her call him pretty! And yet. Any kind words from her lips brought joy to his heart.

He stood, and she sketched, and so the morning passed. On his way back to his rooms, Benedick wondered what kind of sketch Beatrice might gift to him. Was a self-portrait too much to hope for?

He caught sight of Don John, and ducked behind a potted fig tree. He was in no humor to have his mood ruined by interacting with that wretched gentleman.

But Don John just continued on toward his own room, looking happier than Benedick had ever seen him.

He did not like the look of that at all.

Beatrice worried all evening over what sketch to present to Benedick. Something romantic, but she had told him truly, she enjoyed the act of sketching, and usually paid little heed to her subjects. Her old works tended to be stuffed into her desk and forgotten. Most were smudged beyond hope. She considered the strawberry blossom that she had recently completed.

How utterly her thoughts had changed from when she had started it!

She set it aside for him, then slipped into her bed.

Hero woke her the next morning, leaping onto her bed and laughing. "Today is the day! I am to be wed! To my dear Claudio, who is a treasure among men."

"Oh, is that today? I had forgotten."

Hero laughed, her eyes bright with joy.

"Has he yet said your words?" Beatrice asked.

A cloud passed over Hero's face, but was quickly dismissed. "That matters not. He loves me, and I chose him. I have always held that we are in control of our own destiny, and that our words are the most nebulous of guidelines."

"Have you always held that?" Beatrice asked.

Hero nodded. "I have. You and I have never discussed our thoughts on soulmarks. I think perhaps both of us would rather think of them as little as possible."

Beatrice had never considered that Hero might be less than delighted with her own words. It was as she'd realized yesterday— her worry over her own soulmark had blinded her to the needs of her much-beloved cousin.

"I have always planned to ask my husband to read them," Hero admitted, her voice soft. "They are not encouraging, and make me question myself," she admitted.

"Mine are more a doom than a fate," Beatrice said. "Or so I have always thought. But perhaps I should follow your temperate example and simply plan to show them to my chosen mate."

"Come on, you two! It is time to be getting you ready!" Margaret bustled into the room, practically glowing. Things must be going well with her beau, as well.

Hero was as lovely as a summer day, clad in her wedding gown. Beatrice wove daisies through her hair, since they were Hero's favorite flower. Margaret painted Hero's face, highlighting her already fine features.

They stood back and admired their handywork. "I think you are ready, Cousin."

Leonato poked his head in, and paused to look at his daughter. "Truly, my darling, you are a vision. Oh, how I wish your mother could be here, today of all days. But come, the prince, the count, Signior Benedick, Don John, and all the gallants of the town are come to fetch you to church."

Beatrice followed along to the church. She allowed herself only a moment to daydream of being married here herself, and she couldn't help a smile when she met Benedick's eyes from across the chapel.

Leonato led Hero forward, smiling. "Come, Friar Francis, be brief. Only to the plain form of marriage, and you shall recount their particular duties afterwards."

Friar Francis, a kindly old man who Beatrice had known her whole life, gave Leonato a patient smile, then turned to Claudio. "You come hither, my lord, to marry this lady.

"No," Claudio said, his voice tight.

Beatrice's uncle gave an awkward chuckle. "To be married to her. Friar, you come to marry her."

Friar Francis gave Claudio an odd look, but continued. "Lady, you come hither to be married to this count."

Hero gave a brilliant smile. "I do."

"If either of you know any inward impediment why you should not be conjoined, I charge you, on your souls, to utter it.

Claudio gave Hero a hard look. "Know you any, Hero?" Beatrice hoped that the count was simply nervous, but his behavior was decidedly odd. She exchanged looks with Benedick, and he looked as confused as she.

Hero's face had gone pale, but her voice was steady. "None, my lord."

"Know you any, count?" the friar asked.

Claudio remained silent.

The moment stretched till Leonato gave another chuckle, this one sounding decidedly forced. "I dare make his answer, none."

At that, Claudio's face went dark with anger. "Oh, what men dare to do! You dare make my answer, do you?"

Benedick stepped forward and put a hand on Claudio's shoulder. "What are you on about?" he asked, his voice low and intense.

Claudio tore out of Benedick's grip. "Stand thee by, friar. Good Leonato, by your leave, will you with free and unconstrained soul, give me this maid, your daughter?"

Leonato nodded. "As freely, son, as God did give her me."

"And what have I to give you back, whose worth may counterpoise this rich and precious gift?"

"Seriously, what are you doing?" Benedick demanded again, louder this time.

Don Pedro stepped forward, forcing Benedick to step back. "Nothing, unless you render her again," the prince said.

"Sweet prince, you learn me noble thankfulness. There, Leonato, take her back again." Claudio moved as if to shove Hero away, but Benedick caught his wrist. "Give not this rotten orange to your friend!" Claudio shouted. "She has but the sign and semblance of her honor. Behold how like a maid she blushes! Oh, with what show of truth can cunning sin cover itself! Would you not swear, all you that see her, that she has given her heart to me? But she has not, and she loves me not, and her heart belongs to another. She has played me for the fool and shattered my own heart to pieces."

Rage simmered through Beatrice's veins in place of blood. She stepped between Claudio and her cousin. How dare he? How *dare* he? To slander Hero so, and in this moment? To meet her with scorn when he should be sweeping her into his loving embrace?

Her uncle stared in horror. "What do you mean, my lord?"

"I do not mean to be married," Claudio declared. "I will not knit my soul to a liar, not when I showered her with bashful sincerity and comely love."

"And was I ever otherwise with you?" Hero asked, her voice faint. She stepped past Beatrice and reached out, as if for Claudio's hand, but he only glared at it as if it were a serpent.

"You seem to me as Diana in her orb, as perfect as is the bud ere it be blown. But you are more intemperate in your blood than Venus."

Hero let her hand drop. "Is my lord perhaps unwell? Were you plagued with fever dreams that seemed real enough that they bring such accusations to your tongue?"

Leonato turned to Don Pedro. "Sweet prince, why speak not you?"

Don Pedro gave Leonato a look as bleak as a January midnight. "What should I speak? I stand dishonored, that I have gone about to link my dear friend to a common stale."

"To a what?" Beatrice snarled. Had they all gone mad? She reached out and took Hero's hand in her own. The girl's skin was like ice, and she trembled like a colt taking its first steps.

Her uncle looked pale. "Are these things spoken, or do I but dream?"

Don John stepped forward, his visage smooth, but Beatrice thought she detected a hint of glee in his eyes. "Sir, they are spoken, and these things are true." He looked like a man surveying a complete victory.

Benedick met Beatrice's eyes. "This looks not like a nuptial."

Hero squeezed Beatrice's fingers. "Well observed, how true," she agreed. Hysteria crept into the edges of Hero's voice.

Claudio ignored her and turned his attention to her father. "Leonato, stand I here? Is this the prince? Is this the prince's brother? Is this face Hero's? Are our eyes our own?"

"All this is so. But what of this, my lord?"

"Let me but move one question to your daughter, and, by that fatherly and kindly power that you have in her, bid her answer truly."

Leonato turned to Hero. "I charge you to do so, as you are my child."

"Oh, how I am beset!" Hero cried. Beatrice's heart ached at the pain in her voice. "You claim you wish an honest answer, but you have already made up your minds what that must be. What is the purpose of this farce?"

Claudio did not look at her, but past her. "To make you answer truly to your name."

"And is my name not Hero? Who can blot that name with any just reproach?"

"What man was he who talked with you yesternight, out at your window betwixt twelve and one?

"I talked with no man at that hour, my lord."

"No, indeed, it was not words you were exchanging," the prince said. "Leonato, I am sorry you must hear, but upon my honor, myself, my brother and this grieved count did see her, hear her, at that hour last night, meet with a ruffian at her chamber-window, who has indeed, most like a villain, confessed the vile encounters they have had a thousand times in secret."

Don John interrupted before the prince could continue, or before Beatrice could exclaim about the impossibility of such a statement. "Fie, fie! Her acts are not to be named, my lord, nor especially to be spoke of on such holy ground. There is not chastity enough in language to utter them without offense. Thus, pretty lady, I am sorry for your misgovernment."

Claudio put one hand over his heart, and his eyes shone with unshed tears. "Oh Hero, what a Hero would you have been if half your outward graces matched the thoughts and counsels of your heart! Was it only by your father's will that you turned your eyes to me? Your eyes, but never your heart, because that already belonged to another.

"Did you search out my words so that you might utter them? Did you think to lead me into marriage and then abandon our shared bed for another? Or did you have darker plans for me? Did you long for a widow's robes? Black would suit you well, you creature of lies and deceit! But fare thee well, most foul, most fair! Farewell to your pure impiety and impious purity! For you I'll lock up all the gates of love, and turn my heart to stone."

Hero let out a piercing scream and swooned. Beatrice caught her, but wasn't able to bear her weight, and they both collapsed in the rustle of Hero's wedding gown.

"Has no man's dagger here a point for me?" her uncle cried.

Beatrice gaped at him. Did he seriously believe this nonsense? Perhaps Hero's accusers had seen something, but she was certain it was not what they believed they witnessed. She turned her attention to Hero. "Darling cousin, I know you are innocent.

Please, you must bear up under this, we will set it right." But Hero lay heavy on her chest, unmoving, her eyes closed.

Don John, standing behind Claudio and Don Pedro, allowed himself a smirk. "Come, let us go. These things, come thus to light, smother her spirits up."

Don Pedro and Claudio turned to follow him, not casting a single look back.

Benedick stayed, and knelt by her side. "How is the lady?"

Beatrice shook Hero's shoulder. "I can't tell if she's breathing." Her heartbeat thundered in her ears. If Hero died of this slander– but no, she must live. "Help, uncle! Hero! Wake up, Hero! Uncle! Benedick! Friar!"

Her uncle collapsed to the ground and buried his face in his hands.

"Hero! Please wake up," Beatrice begged.

The friar knelt beside her and took Hero's hand. "Have comfort, lady."

"Does she live?" Beatrice asked.

Friar Francis gave her a gentle smile. "Why should she not? It is only a swoon, she shall be well."

Leonato sprung to his feet and began pacing. "Would the two princes lie, and Claudio lie, who loved her so? And yet, I know my daughter, and trust in her goodness to the core of my soul. She looked upon Claudio with earnest eyes and a gentle heart. And yet I owe the prince my loyalty. And yet he has purposefully injured my only and beloved child. My loyalties are torn in twain, and I know not how to proceed."

Benedick stood and moved to Leonato's side. "Sir, I know not what to say. But I must protest that the whole of it is suspicious, and their accusations too wild to be believed."

Beatrice hugged Hero close. "On my soul, my cousin is belied!"

Benedick nodded, belief in her in every line of him, and Beatrice had to blink back grateful tears. "Lady, were you her bedfellow last night?"

Beatrice shook her head. "No, truly not, although, until last night, I have this twelvemonth been her bedfellow."

"That is proof enough for me," said Benedick.

Friar Francis stepped forward and grabbed Leonato's shoulders. "Listen to me. I have known this girl since infancy, and know as surely as her cousin that these accusations are baseless. Let any man call me a fool if you will, but trust not my reading nor my observations, trust not my age, my reverence, my calling, nor my divinity, if this sweet lady lies not guiltless here, under some biting error."

Leonato shook his head. "Friar, she has yet not denied it. Could not her swoon indicate guilt? And yet I cannot believe it."

"She has only not denied it because she has been given no chance to," Beatrice said. "She knew that Claudio and the Prince wouldn't listen."

Friar Francis left Leonato and returned to Beatrice and Hero. He laid a hand to Hero's forehead, and her eyes fluttered open. "There you are, my child," he said. "Welcome back."

Tears slipped out of Hero's eyes, unchecked, and soaked into Beatrice's dress. Beatrice herself had started weeping when she feared Hero dead and could not seem to stop, though she did manage to keep her tears quiet.

"Lady, what man is he you are accused of?" the friar asked.

Hero sat up slowly, as if she didn't trust her own body. "They know who do accuse me. I know not. I know no more of any man alive than that which maiden modesty allows! If any proof exists that I met with any strange man, or that I yesternight exchanged a single word with any creature, you may refuse me, hate me, torture me to death!"

Friar Francis nodded. "There is some strange misunderstanding in the princes."

Benedick frowned. "Two of them have the very bent of honor, and if their wisdoms be misled in this, the practice of it lives in Don John, whose twisted spirit toils in villany."

Leonato knelt next to Hero and took her hand between his. "They wrong her honor, and the proudest of them shall well hear of it. But how will we prove the truth? "

Friar Francis hummed thoughtfully. "The princes left your daughter for dead. Let her be hidden and publish it that she is dead indeed. Maintain a mourning ostentation, and on your family's old monument hang mournful epitaphs and do all rites that appertain to a burial."

Leonato frowned. "What shall become of this? What good will that do?"

"This act, well carried out, shall on her behalf change slander to remorse. Her dying, as it must so be maintained, upon the instant that she was accused, shall be lamented, pitied, and excused by every hearer. For that which we have, we prize not, but being lost, we find the virtue in it. So will it fare with Claudio. When he hears she died upon his words, the idea of her life shall sweetly creep into his study of imagination."

"Signior Leonato, let the friar advise you. And though you know my inwardness and love are very much due unto the prince and Claudio, by my honor, I will deal in this on your behalf," Benedick said.

Leonato brushed a tear away from Hero's cheek, then took her face between his hands. "How like your mother you look. Do you swear to me that you are falsely accused?" he asked. "Before you answer, know that even if you are not, you are still my daughter, and I will still love you."

Hero nodded. "I do swear, Father. I am falsely accused."

"Very well," Leonato said. "I am sorry I doubted you. I let myself be ruled by fear and anger. Your cousin and the friar are right. I should have instantly known that such accusations could be nothing but vile falsehoods. It was my pledge to the prince that led me to doubt, and I am sorry to have added to your pain in this dark moment."

Hero took her father's hand, and he helped her to her feet. "Let us tell one and all that my daughter is dead," Leonato said.

Friar Fracis took Hero's other hand. "Come, lady, die to live. This wedding-day perhaps is but prolonged. Have patience and endure." He led Leonato and Hero away. When Beatrice went to follow, Benedick caught her elbow.

"Lady Beatrice, have you wept all this while?"

"Yes, and I will weep a while longer, I fear."

Benedick wiped away her tears, his hands warm and gentle. "I do not desire that."

"I do it freely, at my own desire."

"Surely I do believe your fair cousin is wronged."

Beatrice nodded. "And how much might the man deserve of me who would right her!"

His thumb still stroked her cheek, even though her tears had finally slowed. "Is there any way to show such friendship?"

"A very easy way."

"May a man do it?"

Beatrice took a slight step back. "It is a man's office, but not yours." She could not ask it of him. She would not divide his loyalty, especially not before she had any real claim to it.

"I find that I do love nothing in the world so well as you. Is that not strange?"

Beatrice let out a sound somewhere between a laugh and a sob. "Strange indeed. Yet it might be possible for me to say that I loved nothing so well as you. But believe me not. And yet I lie not. I confess nothing, nor deny nothing. I am worried for my cousin, and she must be my focus now."

Benedick's expression could not be called a smile. It was a look of pure wonder. "By my sword, Beatrice, you love me."

"Do not swear my love by your sword."

"I will swear by it that you love me, and I must confess that I love you. And do it with all my heart."

"This is neither the time nor place for confessions, but I love you with so much of my heart that none is left to protest."

Benedick picked her up and twirled her around before setting her on her feet again. "Come, bid me do anything for you."

Beatrice was dizzy and overwrought, and found herself speaking the words she'd dare not even think. "Kill Claudio."

Benedick flinched. "Kill Claudio? No. Not for the wide world."

Beatrice's heart ached. Love was a terrible thing, a suffering from which there was no escape. "You kill me to deny it. Farewell." She turned to go.

Benedick caught her wrist. "Wait."

She tugged at his grip, but he was too strong. "I am gone, though I am here. I pray you, let me go."

"Beatrice—"

"Let me go."

"Claudio is my friend. He once was more, and I still love him well."

Beatrice finally managed to free her wrist from his grasp. "You cannot love both me and my enemy."

"Is Claudio your enemy?"

"Is he not approved in the height of villainy, that has slandered, scorned, and dishonored my kinswoman? Sweet Hero! She is wronged, she is slandered, she is undone."

Benedick reached toward her, palm up. "Beatrice, by this hand, I love you."

"Then use it for my love some other way than swearing by it."

He hesitated. "Do you think in your soul Count Claudio has wronged Hero?"

"Yes, as sure as I have a thought or a soul. Would that I were a man! I would eat his heart in the marketplace."

Benedick gasped. He closed his eyes and took a deep, slow breath. "Enough. I am engaged. I will challenge him."

Beatrice found that both of her hands had traveled to her lips. "Benedick," she whispered. Too many feelings warred in her breast, but she pushed up her sleeve and unwound her armband, while he did the same.

She could hardly see his words through her tears. She traced the lines on his skin. "Perhaps I should be sorry, that I have marked you with such darkness. But I will not be. As you are mine, I am yours, and all that we felt in the past is done. There will only be love between us now."

Benedick caressed her arm, his gaze devouring her words in turn. "My love for you will burn all that stands against us, and your enemies are mine. I will kiss your hand and leave you. And by my hand, Claudio shall render me a dear account. As you hear of me, so think of me. Go comfort your cousin. I must say she is dead." He traced her words one last time and left her.

"Benedick!" she called after him, suddenly afraid of all she might lose. "Are you confident that you can defeat him?"

Benedick laughed. "Count Claudio has not bested me once."

She pulled her folded sketch from her sleeve. "I brought this for you. Take it, as a token of my love for you."

He kissed the folded paper. "Fear not, I will return to you. No force under heaven could stand against me now."

Benedick paused to rewrap his armband with shaking hands and tuck Beatrice's sketch in a pocket against his heart. A strawberry blossom, perfectly formed and lovingly sketched.

He thought back to the moment when Beatrice had said his words. How they seemed to echo in his ears. He had feared the words on his skin for so long, feared what they said about his soulmate, about him. And he was indeed mad to fall fully into love at such a moment, but it was irrevocable now. He was her creature, and his wonder at it overrode any other feeling.

He had offered to do anything for her, and could not deny her her vengeance.

But he did also believe that she was right, and that his mission, though dark and violent, was one of justice. A servant girl rushed up to him. "Have you seen the Lady Beatrice? Don John has left, and she is much required back at the estate."

"She is just inside," he said. "Do you wish for me to wait and walk you both back?"

The servant shook her head. "No, my lord, we will find our own way."

Don John fled, eh. Suspicious that. But not at all surprising.

He met Claudio and Don Pedro just outside of Leonato's door. They turned to him with smiles, which he did not return. "Welcome, Signior," said Don Pedro, laughter in his voice, "you are almost come to a fray."

Claudio had the nerve to laugh. "We almost had our two noses snapped off by an old man without teeth."

Don Pedro smirked. "Leonato sought to challenge us both. What do you think about that? Had we fought, I doubt we should have been too young for him." Was the man joking? Had they not been told that Hero was dead? And yet here they were, laughing at her father?

Any regrets Benedick had were falling away, crumpling to ash in the face of their mirth. "In a false quarrel there is no true valor. I came to seek you both."

Claudio grinned at him. How had he ever felt any fondness for this callous boy? "We have been up and down to seek you.

For we are overwrought with melancholy and would fain have it beaten away. Wilt thou use thy wit?"

"It is in my scabbard," Benedick said, his voice flat. He remembered Beatrice calling him the prince's fool and seeing the truth of it in Claudio and Don Pedro's eyes stung much sharper than the original barb. "Shall I draw it?"

Don Pedro arched his eyebrow, seeking a jest. "Do you wear your wit by your side?"

"Never any did so, though very many have been beside their wit," Claudio said.

Don Pedro finally frowned. "As I am an honest man, he looks pale. Are you sick or angry?"

"What has he to be angry about? I am the one who has today been most wronged. I truly thought she loved me, and I thought I loved her in return."

Benedick could only gape. Claudio most wronged? He was glad he knew that Hero was not truly dead, or he might have lost all control and gone straight for the whelp's throat.

The prince leaned forward. "By this light, he changes more and more. I think he be angry indeed."

Benedick met Claudio's eyes squarely. "You are a villain. I jest not. I will make it good how you dare, with what you dare, and when you dare. Do me right, or I will protest your cowardice. You have killed a sweet lady, and her death shall fall heavy on you. Let me hear from you."

"I do not understand this joke," Claudio said. "But surely you are not serious. You heard what we all witnessed. And you and I—we are friends, are we not? It is not possible that you could side against me in this."

"We must needs lighten the mood," the prince said. "I'll tell thee how Beatrice praised thy wit the other day—"

"You keep her name out of your mouth," Benedick snapped.

"Are you truly choosing her over me?" Claudio said. He sounded as if he might cry. His eyes flicked to Benedick's arm, and froze. "Your armband. I can make out its outline. It is crooked. I have never seen it less than perfectly positioned."

Benedick laid his hand over his words. "Beatrice spoke my words, and I spoke hers." In spite of his current company, he couldn't help but smile as he spoke. That he might shout it from the rooftops!

"That cannot be," Claudio said. "It was all a joke–it was the prince's plan that you might hear us in the garden, not a word we said was true."

Benedick shrugged. "Beatrice is my soulmate, and I am her man. There can be no doubting it. Now. Fare you well, boy. You know my mind. My lord, for your many courtesies I thank you. I must discontinue your company. Your brother has fled from Messina, and I have little doubt this whole tragedy stems from trusting his word. You have among you killed a sweet and innocent lady. For my Lord Lackbeard there, he and I shall meet. Till then, peace be with him."

Benedick entered the gate, then paused just out of sight to listen to their response.

"He is in earnest," Don Pedro said.

"In most profound earnest. And for the love of Beatrice." Claudio sounded stunned.

"He has challenged you."

"Most sincerely."

Their silence stretched. Benedick waited for the sounds of their footsteps moving away, but they seemed to be standing still. Possibly staring at each other in shock.

"Wait," Don Pedro said. "Did he not say that my brother has fled? This must be looked into."

At that, they finally hurried off.

Benedick went to question the servants on Don John's movements. He would discover what part the prince's brother had played in all this, and make sure that all was revealed.

Beatrice went through Don John's room, making sure he hadn't stolen anything and looking for any clues he might have left behind, anything that might help her clear Hero's name.

There were some scraps of partially-burnt paper that she'd held some hopes of, but those were all poorly composed poetry about the nature of solitude.

When that task was done, and failed, she went to see her cousin, and offer what comfort she might. Hero had stripped off her wedding dress and thrown it into a corner. She lay on her back in her bed, staring up at the ceiling, one hand covering her armband.

"I cannot believe I fainted," Hero said. "And now I have to pretend to have died of heartbreak." She heaved a sigh. "Though I must admit that heartbreak is the shape of things."

"Perhaps he is not your destined match," Beatrice said. "He never said your words."

Hero gave a sharp laugh. With sudden manic energy, she sat up and tore her armband off, flinging it onto the pile with her crumpled gown. "For you I'll lock up all the gates of love, and turn my heart to stone," she said, without looking. "That is why I screamed. That is why I swooned. Because he said those words, those words that I have so long hoped and feared to hear, at the very moment of his repudiation. How can I love him who has done this to me? How can love exist without trust? Why would he and the prince decide to so publicly shame me? Even were their lies truth, how could they be so cruel? Claudio is no virgin. Lord knows I am, but even were I not, I would still be human, still deserve to be treated with some care. I have been true to him, and would have been true to him for my entire life, but he did not even give me a chance to stand against his accusations. And yet, by these cursed marks on my skin, I must love him. But I must also hate him."

"I have charged Benedick to kill him," Beatrice said.

Hero looked up at her, her eyes grim. "Good."

A faint knock sounded at the door, and Margaret came in. Her eyes were red, her whole body shaking. "My ladies, I have something that I have to tell you," she said.

Benedick learned that Don John had wasted no time, that he had fled straight from the shattered wedding. His men had begun packing as soon as their lord left for that ill-fated ceremony, and had slipped away to town.

Rumor had them still there, gathering supplies for a journey. Benedick traced their steps, till he came to the tavern, where Borachio and Conrade sat over their cups.

He crept in and took a table behind them, listening in hope that he might overhear something incriminating.

"You mustn't be angry with me," Borachio said. "You know that it was on our lord's behest that I wooed Margaret. She means nothing to me. Less than nothing. The only thing about her that matters is her status as the Lady Hero's gentlewoman."

"And her lovely hair and figure, that she might be mistaken for her mistress," Conrade said. "Do you think I am blind? I remember your dearly departed wife. She was of a similar type. Do you really expect me to believe that you could woo a woman so like her and feel nothing?"

"I do expect you to believe it. It is the truth."

"We agreed that our situation would not necessarily be exclusive, but we also vowed to consult with each other before pursuing another! You sought to frame the innocent Hero as a cheat by being a cheat yourself," Conrade snapped.

Benedick buried his face in his hands. He had already heard enough. Had the prince and Claudio really believed that one of Don John's constant companions had just happened to be the one they caught sight of when the bastard brought them to see proof of Hero's transgressions? Did they have rocks where their brains should be?

Still, there would be time to educate the prince and count later. Now was a moment for action. He stood and drew his sword. "You two are going to come with me," he said. "There are those who much need to hear your story."

Beatrice took Margaret's confession to Leonato, and had just finished explaining the truth of the situation to her uncle when Benedick, his blade naked in his hand, pushed two men into her uncle's office. Both men were bruised and bloody, and Benedick pristinely untouched.

Benedick paused a moment to smile at Beatrice, and the sight warmed her heart. She could not help but smile at him in return.

Then Benedick turned to her uncle, his expression again grave. He looked well, so serious and steady. "I have brought these lying knaves to give testimony, for their offenses against the very ideas of honesty and decency are great indeed."

"We've had the truth of it from Margaret," Leonato said. "But let us drag these villains to the prince and let them give their confession to him."

"A splendid idea," Benedick said. His eyes flicked to his prisoners. "Move."

They hurried to obey, fear of Benedick obvious in every line of their bodies.

She followed them to a courtyard, where Don Pedro, with Claudio at his elbow, was overseeing his men as they readied to depart.

"On your knees," Benedick snapped, and Don John's two men collapsed to the ground. They crawled away from Benedick, who finally sheathed his sword, to grovel at the prince's feet.

Borachio knelt at Don Pedro's feet. "Sweet prince, I am here to give confession. I have deceived even your very eyes. It was your brother, Don John, who incensed me to slander the Lady Hero, for he could not bear to see her and Claudio joined together in love and joy. It was his plan that you should be brought into the orchard, where you saw me court Margaret in Hero's garments, and you followed his will in how you disgraced her when you should have married her." He sagged, and cast a frightened glance at Benedick, who stood glowering, his arms crossed over his chest. "My villainy is upon record. The lady is dead upon mine and my master's false accusation. I desire nothing but the reward of a villain."

Beatrice watched with satisfaction as every drop of blood seemed to drain from Claudio's face. Don Pedro looked stricken, too, as he turned to his young companion. "Runs not this speech like iron through your blood?"

"I feel like I have drunk poison while he uttered it." Claudio did sound quite sick, which pleased Beatrice endlessly.

Don Pedro turned his attention back to Borachio, who had dared not move from his crumpled position on the ground. "You swear that my brother set you to this treachery?"

"He did. And I did it out of love for him, for he can smile only at the misery of others." He glanced at his companion, who had remained silent. "But Conrade is innocent in this, pray do not punish him for my actions. Margaret as well is innocent. For she knew not what she did when she spoke to me and has always been just and virtuous in anything that I do know by her."

It was unexpected, that he should hope to spare Margaret or his companion. Beatrice would still fain see all of them but poor Margaret burn, the prince and count not excluded.

Leonato waved to one of the guards who had followed from his office. "Take these two away. We shall decide on their punishment later."

As the two men were dragged away, Claudio fell to his knees and buried his face in his hands. "Sweet Hero! She did love me. Enough to die of it. What have I done?"

"It took but a little effort to search out the truth," Benedick said, looking down at Claudio and giving him much the same look that he'd given Borachio and Conrade. "Perhaps an attempt should have been made before you slandered an innocent lady."

"Indeed," Leonato said, his voice acid. "I thank you, prince, count, for my daughter's death. Record it with your high and worthy deeds, for it was bravely done, if you bethink you of it."

Claudio wept into his hands, and Beatrice rejoiced to see it. "I know not how to pray your patience," he managed, his voice weak and watery. "Yet I must speak. Choose your revenge yourself. Impose me to what penance your invention can lay upon my sin."

Don Pedro knelt by Claudio's side. "To satisfy you, I would bend under any heavy weight that you'll enjoin me to."

"I cannot bid you bid my daughter live. That is impossible. But, I pray you both, tell the people in Messina how innocent she died. And if your love can labor ought in sad invention, hang her an epitaph upon her tomb and sing it to her bones tonight.

"Prince, I would have your vow that your brother will pay for for his crimes in blood.

"Count, as for you, tomorrow morning come you to my house, and since you could not be my son-in-law, be yet my nephew. My brother has a daughter, almost the copy of my poor Hero, and she alone is heir to both of us. Give her the right you should have given her cousin, and so dies my revenge."

Beatrice gaped at her uncle. What madness was this? To let the wretch off with a song? To allow him still to marry Hero, for they had no other mysterious cousins to produce. Had her uncle discussed this with Hero herself, or was she simply being handed over, even after such a rank betrayal, with not a care to her preference?

Don Pedro gave her uncle a grim nod, and Claudio stared up at him with tears streaming down his face. "Oh noble sir, your over-kindness wrings tears from me! I do embrace your offer."

Her uncle looked down at the boy, and Beatrice could not read his face. "Tomorrow then I will expect your coming. Tonight I take my leave." He followed in the direction the guards had taken.

Benedick gave Claudio one last cold look, then turned to Beatrice. He extended his hand, and she took it. For a moment, all fell away but him, and joy flitted like a butterfly in her heart.

Claudio gasped and looked like he had been punched. Benedick acted like he didn't exist, and pulled Beatrice away.

"What has passed between you and Claudio?" she asked.

"Claudio undergoes my challenge, and either I must shortly hear from him, or I will subscribe him a coward. I pray, tell me for which of my bad parts did you first fall in love with me?"

Beatrice sagged with relief. Benedick had not failed her. If Hero did not wish to spend her life joined to Claudio, he would be her escape. She squeezed his hand. "For them all together, they maintained so politic a state of evil that they will not admit any good part to intermingle with them. But for which of my good parts did you first suffer love for me?"

He laughed, and she loved the sound of it. "Suffer love! A good epithet! I do suffer love indeed, but for a single one of your smiles I suffer it gladly. Tell me, how is your cousin?"

"Very ill."

Benedick paused, and turned to face her. His free hand brushed against her cheek. "And how are you?"

Beatrice blinked away sudden tears. "Very ill too. Even with all sorted and discovered, I cannot find it in me to forgive."

Benedick nodded. He brought the back of her hand to his lips and pressed a kiss there. "Love me and mend. Go to your cousin, and let her know all that we have learned, and what your uncle has planned."

Beatrice did not want to let go of his hand. "I do love you," she said. "Would you marry me, Benedick?"

"I had thought to ask you that."

"Then we are in agreement, and will be married."

Benedick kissed her. It was dizzying. "As you say, my dearest heart."

She leaned her head on his chest and listened to his heartbeat. "Without you, in all this, I would have been lost."

He shook his head. "You can weather any storm, with or without me. But it will never have to be without me again."

"Then come with me," she said.

Benedick swept her into his arms. "I will live in your heart, die in your lap, and be buried in your eyes. And moreover, I will go with you to your cousin."

Benedick stood quietly as Beatrice recounted all to Hero.

"So my father wills that I marry Claudio in the guise of this new cousin," Hero said. "But I might go swiftly from wife to widow, if it be my will?"

"I have challenged him," Benedick said. "He is no match for me in a fight."

After seeing how he'd handled Borachio and Conrade, Beatrice could not doubt him. "If it were up to me, I would choose revenge," she said. "But the choice must be yours, cousin. For it is you who were wronged. And you who loves him."

"I would have words with Cupid, were he to dare show his face. Forgiveness is a rocky path, and love an unreliable staff to use as a guide upon it. Look how forgiveness has treated Don Pedro in regards to his brother." She sighed. "Does Claudio suffer in thinking me dead?"

"Once the truth was revealed, he did suffer indeed," Benedick said.

"And he will be much glad to see me alive again," Hero mused. "I will be entering our union from a position of strength."

"Indeed, it may be many a year before he should dare cross you in even the smallest of things," Benedick agreed.

Hero looked at Beatrice. "Cousin, would you think me too soft if I do forgive him?"

Beatrice sighed. "Look at this man whom I have accepted. I have no room to judge any other."

"Should I go release the poor boy from my challenge, then?" Benedick asked. "I shall do so only if you are sure, cousin."

Hero smiled at him. "I do like to hear you call me cousin. And I like to see you both so happy. And for some small part of that I must thank Claudio and Don Pedro, so yes. I will open my heart and let all resentment flow out and allow only love to flow back in."

"On your command, cousin," Benedick said with a bow, then he left them.

Beatrice gave her cousin a flat look. "What is this about Claudio and the prince having a part in my romance with Benedick?"

Benedick's heart felt lighter than it ever had before. He had been released from his pledge to kill Claudio. Beatrice loved him, and he her. Don John was fled, and would, if the fates were kind, never show his face in front of Benedick again.

He found Claudio at Hero's fake tomb, tears still streaming down his face. He wished he'd brought some water to share with the boy, for he must be nearing dehydration.

Claudio unrolled a scroll and read from it.

"Done to death by slanderous tongues
Was the Hero that here lies:
Death, in guerdon of her wrongs,
Gives her fame which never dies.
So the life that died with shame
Lives in death with glorious fame.
Hang thou there upon the tomb,
Praising her when I am dumb.
Now, music, sound, and sing your solemn hymn."

Benedick was no judge of poetry, but found that barely passable, at best. Still, it was read with great feeling, as Claudio's tears had yet to slow.

Next, Claudio launched into miserable song. Benedick wished there was some way for Hero to see this performance, for he thought it would please her. She was not nearly as fierce as her beloved cousin, but he knew it had cost her to let go and forgive. Some laughter at Claudio's expense would surely be a balm to the lady's soul.

Claudio finally finished. "Your wailings would certainly put all of the local cats to shame," Benedick said.

Claudio whirled around, startled.

"Fear not, boy. I am not here to end you. I release you from my challenge. I do not clear you of wrongdoing, but as you are to marry, I will not make your future wife a widow."

"Are you to marry as well?" Claudio asked.

"She did ask me, and I agreed to make her the happiest of women."

"I can scarce believe it," Claudio said. He sighed and wiped his face. "What a week this has been."

Don Pedro joined them, his face solemn. It seemed the past days had aged him years. "Come Claudio, let us hence, and don again our wedding clothes, and then to Leonato's we will go."

"I will see you at the church," Benedick said, and watched them go. Just days ago, he would have been at their side, but that was no longer his place.

He went to find Leonato and Friar Francis.

The father was serene, and some would say smug. "Did I not tell you she was innocent?"

Leonato had to acknowledge this with a nod. "But so are the prince and Claudio, who accused her because of Don John's misleading actions. But now all is sorted, and the prince has vowed to capture and punish his wayward brother, so all will be well."

Benedick approached the pair, feeling a twinge of nervousness. "Friar, I must entreat your pains, I think."

The priest gave him a knowing look. "To do what, Signior?"

"To bind me, or undo me. One of them. Signior Leonato, the truth is, your niece regards me with an eye of favor."

Now Leonato looked smug. "That eye my daughter lent her, it is most true."

Benedick would let Beatrice deal with her family as she would. For his part, he could not be angry at their interference, for though it was done in sport, it was also kindly meant. "And I do with an eye of love requite her."

"The sight whereof I think you had from me, Claudio, and the prince. But what's your will?"

"My will is your good will may stand with ours, this day to be conjoined in the state of honorable marriage. In which, good friar, I shall desire your help."

Leonato clapped a hand to his shoulder. "My heart is with your liking."

The friar clapped his other shoulder. "And my help. Here comes the prince and Claudio."

They wore the same outfits as they had at the previous ceremony, but much different faces. Don Pedro still looked grim and sad, and Claudio sad and determined.

"Good morrow to this fair assembly," said Don Pedro.

Leonato nodded. "Good morrow, prince. Good morrow, Claudio. We here attend you. Are you yet determined today to marry?"

"I am."

The door to the chapel behind them opened, and two veiled ladies stepped out. Benedick knew them to be Hero and Beatrice. Claudio looked upon them like enemy soldiers that he stood before naked and unarmed. "Which is the lady I must seize upon?" he asked.

Hero stepped forward. She was steady and calm, clad now in a much simpler dress than her previous gown. "I am sorry, Father, but I am not ready to be married today," she said, removing her veil. She was wearing spectacles, but could not be mistaken for any other. "I fear that I do love Count Claudio, though it is against my better judgment, but he must prove himself to me before I will join myself to him."

Don Leonato did not look surprised by this, and Benedick wondered if he had set the whole charade up so Hero could publicly reject Claudio.

"Hero?" Claudio whispered, elegant tears leaking from the corners of his eyes.

"Nothing certainer," Hero said. "One Hero died defiled, but I do live. And surely as I live, I have been true." That last she said a little tartly.

"But she was dead," Don Pedro said.

"She died, my lord, but while her slander lived," Leonato said.

Claudio fell to his knees. "I will dedicate every portion of my being to proving myself to you, Sweet Hero. And if I am both fortunate and true, then perhaps we shall have a third wedding day."

Hero smiled down at him. "Perhaps. They do say that the third time is the charm."

Beatrice stepped forward while everyone's eyes were on Hero and Claudio, pulling off her veil so she could meet Benedick's eyes. "Did you know of their plots against us? That they sought to trick us into love?"

"Claudio did confess it. He meant it as a bar to pry me away from you, but no matter how our feelings started, no man may deny the truth of our fate. Especially not I."

Beatrice's grumpy expression, especially when turned against someone else, was a gem that he would treasure. "Hmph. I do not like being toyed with. But if my cousin can forgive this day, then so should I. Did you speak with my uncle and the friar?"

Benedick nodded. "I have received their blessing. Shall we marry today? Or would you prefer to wait?"

"I am not a patient woman," Beatrice said. "I would have you now."

Benedick grinned as he took her hand.

Sometimes, when Beatrice first woke up in the morning, her joy filled her so completely that it was hard to breathe. It was a fierce joy, huge and wondrous and endless. She allowed herself to trace the words on her husband's skin. The words that had proved that she mattered more to him than any other.

On such mornings, she let herself wallow in her happiness for the space of three breaths. Then she would wake Benedick with a kiss, for she knew he did not like to wake alone. Then together, they would get up and face their day.

She was perfectly happy.

END

Acknowledgements

I'd like to thank Paul Stefko, as always, for his help and support; Todd Sanders for all of his work on the layout and cover; and my critique group: Anne Leonard, Aimee Picci, Laura Pearlman, and Hammond Diehl. Thank you for always being there to tell me what works and what doesn't.

Thank you to Kickstarter Backers

Thank you so much to everyone who backed the Kickstarter campaign to make this book happen.

Don and Debbie Lackey
Chris Aumiller
Jessica Carver
John R. Muth
Todd Sanders
Richard Novak
Thomas J. Griffin
Laine Wilson
Mark Boudreau
Elizabeth
Vince Baverso
Julie Tennis
Brooke Ardile
Isaac E. Payne
Greg Clumpner
Juliana H-B
Jeff Pepper
Betsy Bodamer
Vicky Boardley
Linda McNair
Bernadette Ulsamer
Beth Shari
Joshua David Bellin
Jenn Scott
Amy Treadwell
Ashley Wygant
Pete Butler
Hilary
Matthew Lackey
Jeanne Cupertino
Kimberly Coombs
Cory Livingston
Alexandra Corrsin
Brandon Ketchum
Andrew Akers
Shannon Keating
Lois Stefko
Phyllis Pigan
Larry Ivkovich

Carissa Lackey
Heather Tatton
Robert Woods Tienken
Tori Hesidence
Deanna
Jonathan Hartz
Nichelle Bauernfeind
Richard
Lisa
Sir Nathan Hargraves
Lori Torone
Julia Mulligan
Frank Oreto
Ross Pollock
Savannah Bozonier
Bill Moran
Mike Brendan
Tracey Levino
Heidi Pilewski
John Thompson
Patrick Ropp
Matt Snyder
Nicholas Kiraly